For all inquiries, please contact us at:
info@puppysmiles.org

To see more of our books, visit us at:
www.PuppyDogsAndIceCream.com

This book is given with love

To

_____

From

_____

Foreward

Anxiety can seem like an enormous beast, looming over everyday life, making even small moments challenging, and preventing full relaxation and enjoyment. Anxiety can feel like climbing a mountain, feeling dizzy, weak at the knees as you scramble to the summit. Feelings of anxiety can be triggered by a variety of experiences such as the stress of returning to school and being separated from families after months of being in very close proximity. In addition to general feelings of anxiety from the pandemic, this separation anxiety triggered from the return to school is a new and unprecedented challenge that both parents and children must face. Just like with adults, it is important to communicate with children and understand what causes their anxiety to rise. We should teach them how to handle their stress, see if their symptoms indicate conditions like General Anxiety Disorder, and also show them that they have a reliable support system in the adults in their lives.

Techniques used by psychotherapists can be useful during these difficult times to both console and build an arsenal of "tools" to cope with these turbulent feelings. Through various types of therapy, the patient and the doctor can get to the root of a person's suffering and find ways to combat the symptoms of anxiety and depression that may arise. With the proper equipment in hand, even the mightiest, most petrifying beast can be defeated.

- Dr. Deisy Boscán

About Dr. Deisy Boscán

Dr. Deisy Boscán is a California licensed psychologist and psychoanalyst, with additional training in pediatric neuropsychology. With nearly 20 years of clinical experience working with children, adolescents, and adults, her expertise ranges from providing both psychoanalytic and psychological treatment for individuals of all ages. Dr. Boscán holds a Ph.D. in Psychology and Post-Doctoral training and certification in psychoanalysis and clinical pediatric neuropsychology.

Dr. Boscán specializes in the developmental assessment of infants and toddlers, as well as neuropsychological assessments and evaluations of learning disabilities for children, adolescents, and adults. Her training and years of experience in the field enable her to ensure accurate identification of central nervous system dysfunctions and developmental disabilities including, but not limited to, intellectual and learning disabilities, autism spectrum disorders, attention deficit/hyperactivity disorders, pediatric head injury, and mood disorders in young children and adolescents.

Coming from a diverse background, Dr. Boscán knows the impact age, education and culture have on an individual's life, so she ensures to take all that into consideration when assessing patients.

Are you fearful of **new things**?
Does **change** make you freeze?

Does the **idea of speeches** make you weak in the knees?

Does your breathing get rapid **before a big test**?

Do you feel like a **failure**,
though you've done your best?

Do **crowds** make you dizzy?
Performance, no way?
Does this agitation
ever get in your way?

This is **Anxiety** and she's **not your friend**. But I promise you'll conquer this beast in the end.

She's **sneaky** and spiky

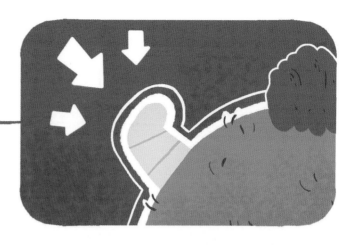

with **razor sharp** claws,

she'll **nibble** your ankles,
she'll **drown** out applause.

She'll **hiss** and she'll **whisper**,
her tongue like a knife,
she'll tell you you're destined
to fail in your life.

She's hungry for

PANIC

she feeds on your sweat -
she **senses your terror**,

but please, don't forget...

So now take a **deep breath**, and count up to **ten**.

Imagine **a feeling of calm**, once again.

Picture **the strength of your will**, deep inside - that will is your **weapon**, and the beast cannot hide.

You're winning, you've got this.
And you'll conquer much more!

You'll leap over the hurdles
that life has in store.

This moment will pass by,
tomorrow will come.

You'll vanquish Anxiety,
you won't succumb.

There'll be times when you stumble,
while you're making your way -
**as long as you're trying,
it will all be okay.**

Claim your FREE Gift!

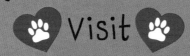 Visit

PDICBooks.com/Gift

Thank you for purchasing

Anxiety Beast

and welcome to the Puppy Dogs & Ice Cream family.
We're certain you're going to love the little gift
we've prepared for you at the website above.